How to make your Felicity Wishes

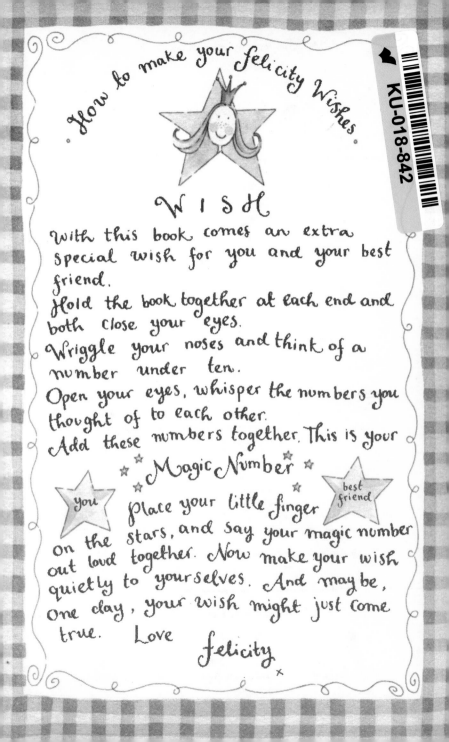

W I S H

With this book comes an extra special wish for you and your best friend.

Hold the book together at each end and both close your eyes.

Wriggle your noses and think of a number under ten.

Open your eyes, whisper the numbers you thought of to each other.

Add these numbers together. This is your

✶ Magic Number ✶

you

best friend

Place your little finger on the stars, and say your magic number out loud together. Now make your wish quietly to yourselves. And maybe, one day, your wish might just come true. Love

felicity

x

For my sister, Anna.
E.V.T

For Jan Rochester – So many handbags, so little time!
H.E.B

Emma Thomson's
felicity Wishes®

FELICITY WISHES
Felicity Wishes © 2000 Emma Thomson
Licensed by White Lion Publishing

Fashion Fiasco text © 2002 Helen Bailey and Emma Thomson
Illustrations copyright © 2002 Emma Thomson

First published in Great Britain in 2002 for WHSmith
This edition published 2005

The rights of Emma Thomson and Helen Bailey to be identified as the authors
and Emma Thomson as the illustrator of this work have been asserted by them
in accordance with the Copyright, Designs and Patents Act 1988.

1

A Catalogue record for this book is available from the British Library

ISBN 0 340 90296 5

Printed and bound in Great Britain by Bookmarque Ltd, Croydon, Surrey.

Hodder Children's Books
A division of Hodder Headline Ltd, 338 Euston Road, London NW1 3BH

CONTENTS

Fashion Fiasco

PAGE 7

Decorating Disaster

PAGE 31

Skating Surprise

PAGE 55

Fashion Fiasco

Felicity Wishes was having a lovely, lazy morning in the garden flicking through the latest copy of *Fairy Girl* magazine. There were lots of really pretty dresses and loads of interesting articles, but the one that had caught her eye was called: 'A Brand New Outfit Equals A Brand New You!' There was a picture of pop star Suzi Sparkle wearing all sorts of dresses, though most of them seemed to be black and none of them had the full skirts Felicity loved so much. Felicity quite liked the *old* her, but a new one sounded interesting. And it was the perfect excuse to go shopping!

"I think," she said to herself out loud as she skipped out of the front door, "that if I'm going to buy a new outfit for a new me, I'll have to go to some new shops!"

So, instead of turning right when she left her house to go down Feather Hill to the shops in Little Blossoming, she turned left and headed up the hill towards Bloomfield. The shops there were well-known for stocking the latest clothes from the hottest fairy fashion designers. Felicity couldn't wait to start trying on the trendiest things!

* * *

First stop was Miss Fairy, described in Felicity's magazine as 'the top shopping experience for the fashion-conscious fairy'.

And there, in the window, was one of the dresses Suzi Sparkle had been wearing in *Fairy Girl*!

Excitedly, Felicity pushed the door open and popped inside.

But, instead of the row upon row of brightly-coloured dresses she'd expected to find, just a few dark-coloured dresses hung in the shadows on matt black rails. Everything was neat, clean and perfect. Felicity felt she was messing up the shop just by being there!

It all seemed quite cold and unfriendly, even down to the fairy assistant who was now heading towards Felicity. She was dressed from head to toe in black, including black wings and a black crown. Even her hair, which was pulled back from her head in a high ponytail, was black. Felicity thought she looked like a giant crow.

"Can I help you?" said the assistant, in a voice which made Felicity think the *last* thing she wanted to do was help.

Shyly, Felicity smoothed down the folds in her skirt, looked up and said as bravely as she could, "I like the dress in the window, but do you have it in pink?"

The assistant looked as if she had swallowed a huge toffee apple in one go.

"We're not stocking *any* pink this year," she said dramatically. "This year, black is the new pink."

Felicity really wanted pink - lilac at a pinch. What was the point of treating yourself to a special outfit if you couldn't buy it in the colour you wanted?

"Don't you have *any* colour other than black?" Felicity asked the crow.

"If madam feels uncomfortable

going straight to black we have other shades such as dark grey, charcoal, midnight black and stormy sky."

"No pink?" asked Felicity.

"No pink," said the assistant firmly. Seeing Felicity's disappointed face, the assistant offered to phone one of their branches to see if they had any pink dresses.

"Tamara? It's Flora from Miss Fairy in Bloomfield. We have a customer here who wants style number 1422 in - " she almost spat out the word, "–PINK!"

Felicity could hear Tamara sniggering down the phone while Flora whispered to her. Felicity thought they were both very rude. Then she remembered the pictures of Suzi Sparkle wearing the black dresses in *Fairy Girl*. Perhaps it *was* time to try something different. She grabbed the dress off the rail, checked the size and said to the assistant (who was still giggling and whispering into the phone), "I'll take this one!"

* * *

Felicity didn't feel as skippy and bubbly as she normally did after buying a dress. In fact, she felt rather flat. It wasn't quite the dress she wanted and it *certainly* wasn't the colour she'd dreamed of. Still, at least she would be at the height of fashion!

She could always dress it up with some sparkly new accessories.

So her next stop was Trinkets, which sold every sort of fairy accessory you could imagine.

The shop assistant in Trinkets was much more friendly than the snooty Flora. When she asked whether she could help Felicity, she seemed to really mean it.

"I'd like a new wand, please," said Felicity.

The shop assistant had spied her shopping bag.

"Ah," she said, "I see you have been to Miss Fairy. You are obviously a very fashion-conscious young fairy."

Felicity was thrilled. That was *exactly* what she was! A fairy with her wand on the pulse of fairy fashion!

"Can I suggest this year's latest look in wands?" said the assistant.

She brought out a terribly thin

and fragile-looking black stick with a blob on the end.

Both Felicity and the assistant stared at it intently.

Finally Felicity asked, "Does it work?"

The assistant looked embarrassed and coughed.

"It's fair to say that some of my customers have found its waving powers to be....

umm.....

limited."

She leaned closer to Felicity and wrinkled her nose. "Between you and me, I'd only carry it on occasions when you know you're not going to need it."

Felicity wondered how she would know in advance whether she needed it or not. She was only a young fairy and hadn't yet left fairy school, but even though she hadn't been granted her own full fairy powers, the wand still looked ridiculously weedy. It was fashionable though, and that was the most important thing.

Next, the shop assistant suggested a new crown to go with the wand, equally small but, Felicity reminded herself, terribly fashionable!

With a new dress, a new wand and a new crown, she might as well go the whole way and get some new wings. As a young fairy she wasn't allowed to have a full pair of wings with a double flutter, but she could choose any pair of single flutter wings she set her heart on.

NAME FELICITY WISHES
CLASS 2/1
HOUSE LOVE HEART
SIGNATURE *felicity Wishes*

In Wings 'N' Things she showed the shop assistant her little Fairy Identity Card and was sent over to the 'Beginner Fairy' wings section.

Felicity thought there had been a mistake as the wings were so tiny. She was a beginner fairy, not a baby one!

She went back to the assistant and showed her ID card again.

"I am at fairy school," she stressed.
"I can have bigger wings."

The assistant was busy sticking
glitter 'go-faster' stripes on her shoes
and didn't look up, but said, "All the
manufacturers have shrunk their
wings this year. Micro wings are the
'in' thing. We can hardly keep up
with demand."

Felicity couldn't remember any of

her friends wearing such teeny tiny wings, and there was something suspicious about the racks and racks of them on display, despite the shop assistant telling her they kept selling out.

She took a pair of the wings off the rack and looked at the swing ticket. "All the power of a standard wing in a simple, stylish design," it read. "For the modern fairy on the move!"

"A modern fairy on the move," she repeated to herself. "That's me! These wings will be just right!"

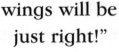

Now all that was left to buy was a new pair of tights.

By this time, Felicity knew better than to ask for pink stripy tights. She *was* a modern fashion-conscious fairy on the move after all!

Proudly swinging her bags, she asked for something she never thought she'd have wanted in a million fairy years. She asked for a pair of black-and-white stripy tights. The assistant gave her a knowing smile and swiftly brought her a pair. "She must recognise me as someone who knows all about fashion," Felicity thought.

Felicity was really exhausted when she got home with all her new things. Some of her purchases may have been small but they still seemed heavy. She

decided to have a big mug of hot
chocolate with extra whipped cream
and sugar to give her an energy
boost. Then she would try on her new
outfit and see what the new Felicity
Wishes looked like.

* * *

Feeling better after her hot
chocolate, Felicity began to unwrap
her goodies. First came the dress
from Miss Fairy, as worn in *Fairy Girl*
by pop star Suzi Sparkle. The dress
was very long and very black. Felicity

looked at the picture of Suzi and then
back at her reflection in the mirror.

Suzi looked beautiful, elegant and
chic draped across a sofa wearing
the dress.

Felicity just looked – and felt – very
uncomfortable. She could hardly
bend down to put on her new tights.
When she did get them on, what a
shock! The tights were indeed black-
and-white as she had asked, but
the stripes weren't going across,
they were going lengthways! Felicity
thought she looked more like a giant
mint humbug than the elegant Suzi
Sparkle.

Things were *not* going according
to plan. The micro wings were so tiny
they kept popping out of her hands.
After a great deal of twisting and
turning she finally got them on.
Time to try them out!

Felicity flew up to the ceiling.

Because the wings were so small
they had to flutter twice as
fast as her usual wings to
achieve the same height.
There was the most
awful buzzing noise
as if a fly was
stuck in the
lamp.

Felicity
looked around.
She couldn't
see a fly, but the
noise continued.
Then she realised it
was coming from her
wings! They were fluttering
so fast they were buzzing. Her
super new micro fashion wings were
making the noise of a monster bee!

* * *

23

Back on the ground, Felicity
unwrapped the thin wand which
wouldn't wave, and tried on the
crown, which was so tiny it kept
slipping off her head.

She looked at herself in the
mirror again.

She had a dress she couldn't
move in.

A pair of wings she couldn't fly in.

A wand she couldn't wave.

A crown that wouldn't stay on.

And a pair of tights which were just… horrible.

The doorbell chimed.

Felicity found she couldn't even walk to the door. Her dress was so long and narrow she had to jump up and down as if she was on a pogo stick. It took such a time for Felicity to get to the door, the bell rang again.

When she opened the door, Polly, Holly and Daisy stared at their friend for a moment before collapsing with laughter.

"What ARE you wearing?" asked Polly, her eyes streaming with tears of laughter.

"Are you off to a fancy dress party?" enquired Holly between fits of giggles.

So Felicity explained about seeing Suzi Sparkle in *Fairy Girl* and how she wanted to be a fashionable fairy on the move, but now she was a fashionable fairy who couldn't move and she really didn't like the new Felicity as much as the old one.

"What has Suzi Sparkle got that I haven't?" asked Felicity who was now laughing as much as her friends.

Holly, who had been reading the article while Felicity told her tale of shopping woe, pointed at the picture of the reclining Suzi.

"No wonder she's draped across a sofa," she said. "She probably can't stand up!"

"She probably *was* standing up but

tripped and landed on the sofa and is now stranded!" shrieked Polly.

When Felicity demonstrated the micro wings with their high-pitched buzz they begged her to stop. They were laughing so much their tummies ached!

Daisy came over to Felicity and put her arms around her. She hugged her so tightly, Felicity's tiny crown popped off.

"Felicity," she said, "we love you just the way you are. We don't *want* a new Felicity, we like the old one!"

"I don't think Suzi Sparkle would be as good fun as you, or such a good friend," added Polly. "It's what's on the inside that counts, not on the outside!"

"What am I going to do with all these things?" said Felicity, looking down at her humbug legs.

"We'll take them back tomorrow," said Daisy. "I'm sure there won't be a problem. In the meantime, you have five minutes to get out of all that black and into something pink and then we'll all go out for an ice-cream!"

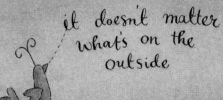

it doesn't matter
what's on the
outside

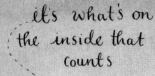

it's what's on
the inside that
counts

Decorating Disaster

Felicity Wishes and her friends
were lolling about on Felicity's bed,
planning what they were going to
do during the half-term break from
the School of Nine Wishes. They had
one week - just long enough to have
masses of fun!

"So," said Polly. "What's it to be? Shopping, shopping or more shopping?"

"I think," said Felicity, looking around her bedroom, "I'm going to re-decorate."

"Does it really need it?" asked Holly, flipping through a magazine without looking up. Decorating was not Holly's idea of fun at all. In fact, anything that required hard work sounded like a very bad idea indeed.

"*Need* doesn't come into it," said Felicity firmly. "I feel like a change."

"It does seem a shame to take down this lovely wallpaper," said Daisy. "It looks almost new to me."

Polly peered up at the ceiling. "I can see a bit of paper peeling - right there, in the corner."

"You see!" exclaimed Felicity triumphantly. "The room does need a make-over!"

"Just stick some glue on it!" said Holly, now becoming worried. "Glue it, let's go shopping and we'll think about decorating later!"

Felicity found some Soopa Doopa glue and Polly flew up to the ceiling to inspect the damage. In one corner there was a tiny piece of wallpaper which had come away from the wall.

"What's it to be, Felicity?" Polly shouted down. "Are we decorating or not?"

Felicity suddenly thought of all the work that needed to be done before the fun could start: moving furniture, taking down posters, removing the curtains, covering up the carpet, cleaning the walls. Even though her friends would help her, perhaps they *should* wait for the long summer holidays.

"Glue it!" shouted Felicity. "We'll leave the decorating for another time."

Holly let out a great sigh of relief and went back to reading magazines.

Polly squeezed a little Soopa Doopa glue out of the tube, but it wouldn't stop. The glue kept on spilling out of the tube in a huge sticky mess. On and on it oozed.

"The glue is going wild! I can't stop it coming out of the tube," she yelled down to her friends.

"Put some on the wallpaper, Pol!" shouted Felicity

"Put the cap back on!" shrieked Daisy.

Holly could feel a headache coming on.

* * *

The glue was getting everywhere. Everything Polly touched seemed to become covered with a layer of super sticky goo.

"I'm flying back down!" called Polly. "There's enough glue up here to stick glitter to every fairy wand in Little Blossoming!"

But as Polly flew down, there was the most tremendous ripping sound.

In amongst the sticky mess, a corner of Polly's right wing had become stuck to the wall. Streaming behind her like a huge paper cape was Felicity's wallpaper!

"Arghh…" shrieked Polly as she landed with a thump on the carpet, the wallpaper floating down and covering her in a huge gooey blanket.

"That's torn it!" said Holly, as the fairies rushed over to their crumpled friend.

With a large strip of wallpaper now covering Polly rather than the wall, there was nothing for it but to redecorate the room after all.

Everyone was already in such a mess that Daisy, Polly and Felicity decided to strip the rest of the wallpaper off the walls there and then, while Holly covered up the furniture with some large white sheets. They used the stars on their wands to prise away bits of wallpaper, then flew about the room pulling off strips like fat paper streamers.

When they had finished, they bundled all the mess into the bin, cleaned themselves up, had a cup of hot chocolate and set off for Do-It-Together to find something special to decorate Felicity's room with.

✳ ✳ ✳

The shop was bustling with fairies
buying paint and paper of every
pattern and colour imaginable.

There was wallpaper with stripes
going up and stripes
going across.
Wallpaper
with big checks
you could play
noughts and
crosses on, and
wallpaper with
checks so tiny
they made
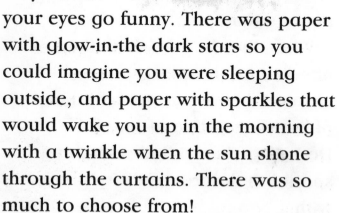
your eyes go funny. There was paper
with glow-in-the dark stars so you
could imagine you were sleeping
outside, and paper with sparkles that
would wake you up in the morning
with a twinkle when the sun shone
through the curtains. There was so
much to choose from!

Then Felicity saw a design she loved.

It was pale pink with enormous deep pink roses the size of dinner plates. Felicity thought it was gorgeous. The others weren't so sure.

"Don't you think the roses are a bit – well – *large*?" said Daisy, looking doubtfully at the design.

"They're humungous!" said Polly. "Far too large for your bedroom, Felicity. How about something more delicate?"

But Felicity was already hugging rolls of the paper. There was no dissuading her.

So the others gathered together some brushes, a bucket, some wallpaper paste and a hard hat for Holly (who was worried about her hair), then set off back to Felicity's house.

The first problem was finding a table long enough for the wallpaper. Holly suggested they used the ironing board which wasn't perfect but, if Daisy held the end of the paper carefully, might just work.

Polly opened the packet of wallpaper paste and sneezed so hard she added too much powder to the bucket of morning dew, making the paste as lumpy as porridge. Even her frantic whisking with the end of her wand didn't appear to make any difference.

Holly cut the wallpaper into a long strip, then put it on the ironing board. Felicity brushed the lumpy paste on to the back of the paper. With so much paste the wallpaper was very heavy and Daisy, Polly and Felicity had trouble lifting it up and flying to the ceiling to hang it.

Holly didn't like heights so she

shouted out instructions
from below.

"Up a bit, left a bit, right
a bit – hang!"

They fluttered up and
down smoothing out the
lumps, then stood back
to admire their handiwork.

The roses were, indeed,
humungous. Daisy had
been right, they were far
too big for Felicity's cosy
bedroom. But, more
worryingly, right in the
centre of the paper was
a huge bulge.

The friends looked at each
other, puzzled.

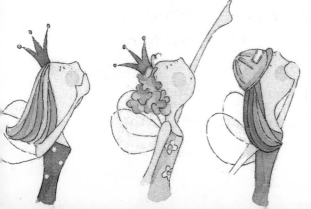

"What is that lump?" asked Holly.

"We smoothed the top, didn't we?" said Daisy to Felicity.

"And Polly and I did the bottom..." said Holly.

But no one had done the middle!

The fairies inspected the lump. It was large, and hard and brush-shaped.

"We've papered over the paste brush!" giggled Felicity.

The friends fell about laughing. Time to start again! But Felicity had had enough of the wallpaper with its huge roses and strange bulges.

"We've only done one sheet, it's been a disaster and I don't like the pattern after all. Let's take it back and get some paint instead."

"But Felicity," chorused her friends, "you've always said you think plain walls are boring!"

"A fairy can change her mind,

can't she?" Felicity replied, gathering up the unused rolls of rose-patterned paper before setting off to Do-It-Together again.

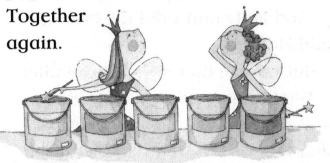

There was an even wider choice of paint colours than there had been of wallpaper patterns, but the fairies knew exactly which colour Felicity would choose. Pink. The question was, which shade?

There was a lovely dusty pink the same colour as Daisy's roses, a fabulous deep pink which Felicity knew would match her duvet beautifully, a delicate light pink that shimmered and was very special, and a pink that reminded Felicity of strawberry ice-cream.

"Oh, they're all yummy! I just don't know which one to choose," said Felicity, as she lined up the tins of paint. She closed her eyes and began, "I spy, with my closed eye..."

Daisy was horrified. "Felicity! You can't choose a colour like that!"

"It's the best way," said Felicity. "There's no such thing as a horrible pink, so whichever one I choose will be perfect."

She shut her eyes and began again, pointing randomly at the tins.

"I spy, with my closed eye, a colour beginning with P!" Felicity's finger stopped on a beautiful pinky lilac colour called 'Twilight Blush'.

It was perfect.

They each got a paint brush, a furry roller, and a pot of white paint for the skirting boards and, for the second time that day, headed back to Felicity's house to start decorating.

Painting was much more fun than papering and the fairies quickly covered the walls with a generous coat of 'Twilight Blush'. They also covered themselves with a layer of paint. The tin said "non-drip" but it didn't say "non-splash" and soon they all looked as if they had a bad case of chicken pox!

After Holly had painted the skirting boards white, they declared the room finished. It looked lovely.

"It's gorgeous, Felicity," said Polly.

"Your method of choosing a colour worked brilliantly after all," agreed Daisy.

Felicity was very quiet.

"Don't you like your new room?" asked Holly wearily. "*Please* tell me that you like it."

"I do," mumbled Felicity, looking down at her toes. What was a little white lie to save her friends' feelings?

But her friends knew her too well and her face said it all. Polly raised one eyebrow in an "are you sure?" kind of way.

"Honestly... I... er... do," said Felicity hesitantly. "It's just after wallpaper, the plain walls look a little... well... *plain*."

This time it was the turn of her friends to remain silent. They stared at her with their paint-splashed faces.

"I mean," said Felicity sensing her friends' despair and beginning to gabble, "I love the colour, but it's just a little... um... *boring*. It needs a pattern."

The fairies groaned. Holly threw herself on to the sheet-covered bed.

"It's at times like this that I'd really love to have graduated from the School of Nine Wishes," she moaned. "If I was a fully-qualified fairy I could just wave my magic wand and instantly transform your room to look however you wanted it. You could change your mind a hundred times and it wouldn't matter."

"Don't you think that might be thought of as a waste of a wish?" said Polly. One of the first lessons they had ever had at fairy school was the importance of using your wishes wisely. Polly wasn't sure that providing Felicity with the right wallpaper and paint counted as a wise wish.

Holly thought for a moment. "The fairy motto starts off saying: I promise to take good care of my wishes. To use them wisely for the good of others. We would be using a wish to help Felicity."

"Are you sure that would be your only reason, though? To help Felicity?" asked Polly, looking worried. "Don't forget, the motto goes on to say: Never to use them for my own gain. And to try my best to live by the Fairy Motto. By changing Felicity's room it means less work for us. Surely that's using a wish for our own gain?"

Daisy suddenly had an idea. "I
know! We can still use our magic
wands to transform Felicity's room,
but without making a wish. Holly,
have you got any white paint left?"

Holly handed over the tin to Daisy,
who carefully dipped the end of the
handle of her wand into the paint
and dabbed it on to the pink wall.
It made a perfect white spot.
She then dipped one of
the points of
the star

in the paint and made eight tiny spots around the first larger spot. She stood back to let Polly, Holly and Felicity see. She had painted a small, white, perfectly formed flower.

"Daisy!" exclaimed Felicity hugging her friend. "That's brilliant! You are so clever."

Daisy turned a sort of 'Twilight Blush' colour and said, "Let's use our wands to cover all the walls."

So the four friends spent the rest of the day dipping and dabbing, painting flowers on the walls with their wands. When they finally finished and the last flower had been painted, Felicity couldn't have been happier. Not only did she have a beautiful pink bedroom, but one where each flower had been hand-painted with care by the friends she loved most. Every single flower would

always remind her how lucky she
was to have such good
fairy friends!

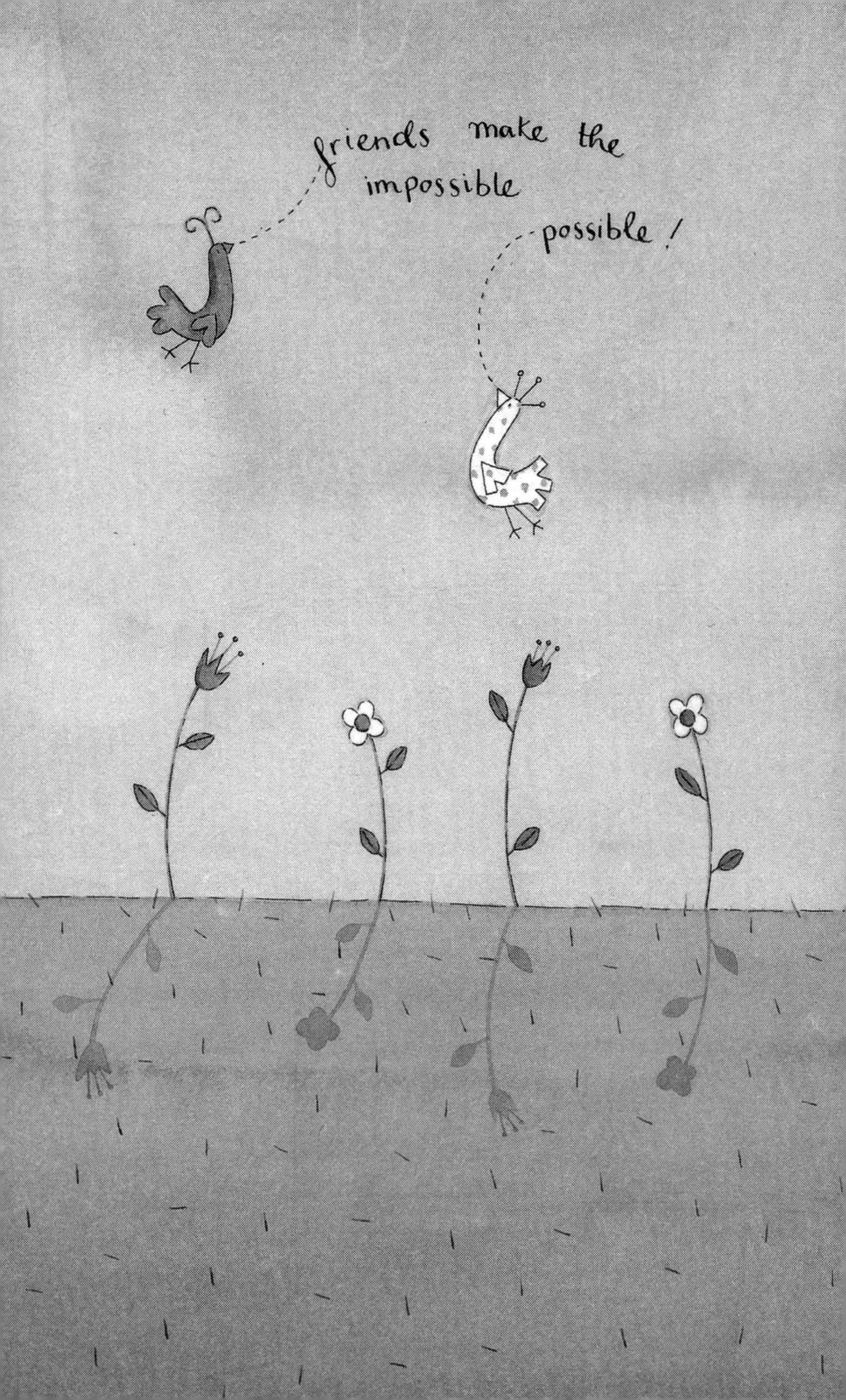
friends make the
impossible
possible !

Skating Surprise

The doorbell chimed several times
before Felicity managed to get to
the door.

"I'm coming! I'm coming!" she
called out. Someone was in a great
rush to see her. When she finally
opened her door, Daisy and Polly
were standing on the doorstep. They
were flushed with excitement and
were carrying their ice-skates over
their shoulders.

"Felicity! Quickly! Find your
skates," said Daisy breathlessly.

"The ice rink has opened for the first time this winter. The queue will be enormous once word gets round."

Polly was equally excited. "If we're quick we can spend the whole afternoon skating," she said. "Holly is meeting us there in twenty minutes."

Skating! Felicity loved skating. She couldn't wait to get on the ice.

"Come in while I find my skates," she said to her friends, who obviously didn't want to waste even a minute of precious skating time.

Felicity started looking for her skates in the hall cupboard, while Daisy chattered on about how lucky it was that she had been to the library to return her book on tropical plants. It hadn't been due back for another few days, but she'd found it so interesting she'd finished it already.

And, if she hadn't returned it early, she would never have passed the ice rink and seen the Frost Fairy putting up an 'Open' sign at the entrance...

✳ ✳ ✳

Felicity's cupboard was jam-packed with all sorts of bits and bobs. There were tennis rackets without strings, but which would make great guitars for a fancy dress party; several pairs of ballet shoes she'd outgrown but couldn't bear to throw away; one Wellington boot, kept in case the other one turned up; an awful orange wand handle, from when she was going through her orange phase; several stars that had no wand handles, but might come in handy one day; and a large umbrella, which would no longer go up, fighting for space with string from the end of a kite which had never come down. Everything, in fact, except a pair of ice-skates.

"I know I've seen them somewhere," she said to her friends, who were hopping up and down trying to conceal their impatience. The question was, where?

"They're probably with your missing welly," said Polly unhelpfully.

Felicity looked in every cupboard she could think of and pulled out every drawer she had. She looked under the bed and found several pairs of tights she thought she'd lost.

She flew up to look on top of the wardrobe and discovered her secret diary, which she'd put in a place so secret even she hadn't been able to find it for weeks.

Behind the sofa she found her half-finished project on Famous Fairies in History, while an inspection of the kitchen cupboard revealed a fairy cake so old it was almost fossilized.

But there was no sign of the skates. Not even a broken lace!

There was nowhere else to look.

"Don't worry," said Daisy, who didn't want to wait any longer. "You can borrow some at the rink."

* * *

The rink was already busy when they arrived. Fairies were rushing around, trying on skates, tightening up laces and making their way to the glistening ice. One fairy was already on the ice speed-skating, turning sharply, spraying tiny ice crystals everywhere.

"Show off," thought Holly, as she waved at her friends. They made their way over to her. Holly was surprised to see that Felicity didn't

have any skates, and raised an eyebrow at her.

"I don't know where my skates have got to," explained Felicity. "I'm just off to borrow some."

It had taken them so long to look for Felicity's skates, the ice rink was now packed. By the time they got to the front of the queue, most of the skates had already been borrowed.

"What size are you?" asked the fairy behind the desk.

"An eighth of a standard wand," said Felicity, peering over the attendant's shoulder at the rows of nearly empty shelves.

"You're out of luck," said the fairy. "The nearest size is a tenth of a compact wand, but that of course comes in a much narrower fitting. It will be far too small for you."

Felicity was determined to skate with her friends.

"It'll be fine," she said confidently. But it was far from fine. The boots were so small she could hardly get her feet into them, even when she reluctantly took off her tights. When she finally got both feet into the boots, she could barely move. Her toes were crinkled up at the end and the laces were too short for her to do them up. And, without her warm tights, her legs began to get hundreds of little goosebumps and turn quite blue. Even Felicity had to admit defeat.

She took them back to the attendant, who eyed her with an "I told you so" sort of expression.

"As you don't have my size, I think it would be better to have boots that are too big rather than too small. I can always wear extra socks!" she said to the attendant, who handed her what seemed like the longest pair of skating boots she had ever seen and a huge bundle of old socks.

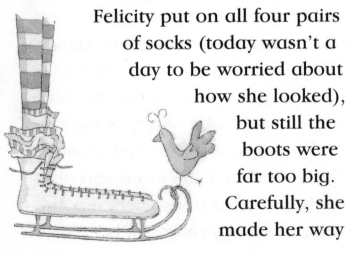
Felicity put on all four pairs of socks (today wasn't a day to be worried about how she looked), but still the boots were far too big. Carefully, she made her way

to the ice. Holly, Daisy and Polly had joined the end of a long line of fairies skating around the rink. Daisy held out her hand and Felicity grasped it to join the line.

At first everything went well. The line snaked around the rink slowly and although Felicity could hardly lift her feet, let alone point them in the right direction, all she had to do was hang on to Daisy. As the fairies got more confident on the ice, though, the faster they skated. Giggling and squealing with delight,

they cut through the crisp ice faster
and faster.

By now, all Felicity could do was
hang on and hope for the best. Her
boots were so heavy and her feet
so long she had no idea in which
direction they were pointing.

Finally, it all got too much. The
line headed towards a corner at top
speed but Felicity couldn't
turn her feet.
The
corner
got
nearer
and nearer
and the line of
skaters got
faster and
faster,

but Felicity's feet felt like long blocks of concrete. As the corner loomed up she shouted, "I've lost control of my feet!" so loudly that Daisy dropped her hand in surprise, and Felicity zoomed straight ahead at such a speed that she shot through the gap in the barrier, across the carpet and landed on a chair in the coffee shop.

The other fairies hurried off the ice to see whether she was all right.

Felicity was fine, just a little embarrassed.

So they sat and drank mugs of steaming hot chocolate and whipped cream, and stared at the size of Felicity's boots. They'd never seen a pair so big and couldn't imagine what sort of a fairy would wear them. Whatever sort of fairy it was, it certainly wasn't Felicity! The boots would have to go back.

"It's such a shame none of us have your size feet," said Holly, "or we could take it in turns to lend you our boots."

Felicity had what she thought was a brilliant idea.

"I could fly above you when you skate so at least I'm not missing out completely. We can still have fun together."

* * *

But Felicity's brilliant idea was not so brilliant in practice.

Daisy, Holly and Polly set off on the ice and Felicity flew just above them.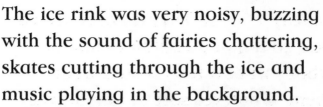
The ice rink was very noisy, buzzing with the sound of fairies chattering, skates cutting through the ice and music playing in the background.

Felicity flew around the rink a few times following her friends but it was too noisy to hear what they were saying. They were chattering and giggling and waving to Felicity. Felicity waved back but really she wanted to hear what her friends were talking about. They seemed to be having such fun!

As Felicity couldn't quite hear what the others were saying, she flew a little lower. She still couldn't

hear, so she flew lower still. So low in
fact, that her skirt covered Daisy's head.
Poor Daisy couldn't see *anything*.
Soon she sent the rest of her
friends sprawling
over the ice.

"Let's all go home," said Polly, dusting the ice off her dress and helping Daisy smooth her crumpled wings. "We can come back another day when Felicity has found her skates."

"I'm so sorry," said Felicity. "I wish I could magic some skates that were the right size."

"Felicity!" exclaimed Polly, slightly shocked. "You know you're not allowed to make wishes for yourself!"

"I don't think saying 'I wish I could' counts," said Holly, who felt rules were made to be broken.

"It might," said Polly who felt rules were there for a good reason, even if you didn't always know what that reason was.

They had only just started practicing simple wishes at The School of Nine Wishes, and then only under the supervision of the Fairy

Godmother. Even so, there had been some disasters. While practicing a wish to stop ice cream from melting, Felicity's ice cream became so frozen that her lips stuck to it when she tried to lick it.

Fairy Godmother had to perform a wish to melt it instantly, which unstuck the ice cream cone, but sent melted ice cream all over Felicity's dress. Everyone but Fairy Godmother thought it was very funny, though

Felicity's lips felt sore for days afterwards.

Felicity was determined her forgetfulness wasn't going to spoil her friends' fun.

"You stay here and I'll go home," she said firmly. "Come back to my house afterwards and we'll toast crumpets."

Felicity unlaced the boots, took out her feet and removed the four pairs of socks. Without her boots, her feet felt as light as whipped cream, though her heart felt a little heavy leaving her friends behind. She could see them sweeping across the ice again, laughing and having fun. A new line of fairies had been formed and they were holding each other around the waist, snaking round the rink.

Still, she reminded herself, as Daisy had said, there would be other days.

* * *

As she was leaving the ice rink, Felicity saw Floella. Floella had already graduated from The School of Nine Wishes and was now a Frost Fairy, responsible for turning winter into spring and autumn into winter. As Floella was older and already a proper fairy with full magic powers, Felicity didn't think Floella would notice her. She wouldn't get simple wishes wrong and certainly not ones involving ice cream!

But Floella *had* seen Felicity and she stopped to talk.

"It's Felicity Wishes, isn't it?" she said. "Are you leaving already?"

Felicity was amazed that Floella had even paused to talk to her, but even *more* surprised that she knew her name. She started to tell Floella about the lost skates, how she thought she might have broken two of the most important fairy rules –

not to use wishes for your own good
and certainly not to use them before
you were qualified to do so – and
about the incident at school when
her tongue got stuck
to the ice cream.

Floella smiled at Felicity kindly.
"All young fairies make mistakes

when they first start at fairy school -
and even when they leave. I know I
do! Don't worry about being perfect.
Just always try to do your best at
everything you do!"

Felicity couldn't believe that
Floella did anything other than
make perfect wishes every time, but
it was nice to know even she had
off days!

"I bet you don't lose your skates,
though," said Felicity.

Floella laughed and looked down
at her own gleaming pair.

"Well no, a frost fairy without
skates would be a disaster! In fact,
I carry a spare pair with me in case
of emergencies. Would you like to
borrow them? They're an eighth of
a standard wand. Do you think they
might fit you?"

"I can't believe it – they're exactly
my size. Can I really borrow them?"

Felicity was jumping up and down with joy.

Floella handed her the skates. "Don't forget to let me have them back!" she said.

As Felicity was thanking Floella, she suddenly remembered where her old skates were!

"I let a young fairy borrow them last year just as I was leaving the ice rink and she must have forgotten to give them back to me!"

Felicity was just about to hurry to join her friends when Floella called out her name. Felicity turned back.

"I'm not recommending you make wishes yet," said Floella, "but sometimes, if it's done with the right intentions, it does no harm." And with that Floella flew off - leaving

Felicity wondering whether she really *had* made a wish for skates, or whether bumping into Floella had just been a happy accident...

Celebrate the joys of friendship with Felicity Wishes!

Felicity Wishes is an extra-special 'friendship' fairy - she's spirited, modern, always there for her friends; she's guaranteed to raise your spirits!

Do you have a friend who you'd like to nominate as your 'best friend'? Do they make you laugh? Are they generous and kind? Why are they your best friend?

Just nominate your best friend and you could see your letter in one of Felicity Wishes' books. Plus the chance to win an exclusive Felicity Wishes prize!

Send in your letter on A4 paper, including your name and age and with a stamped self-addressed envelope to...

Felicity Wishes Friendship Competition,
Hodder Children's Books, 338 Euston Road,
London, NW1 3BH

Australian readers should write to...
Hachette Children's Books
Level 17/207 Kent Street, Sydney, NSW 2000

New Zealand readers should write to...
Hachette Children's Books
PO Box 100-749 North Shore Mail Centre
Auckland, New Zealand

Closing date is 31st March 2007

ALL ENTRIES MUST BE SIGNED BY A PARENT OR GUARDIAN TO BE ELIGIBLE
ENTRANTS MUST BE UNDER 13 YEARS
Winners will be notified by post, and at the latest within 3 months after closing date.
Winners' letters will be published in a future Felicity Wishes book.
The prize will be a Felicity Wishes product we have in stock which we hope you will enjoy
For full terms and conditions visit www.felicitywishes.net/terms

Exclusive Felicity Wishes Prizes!

From January 2006, there will be a Felicity Wishes fiction book publishing each month (in Australia and New Zealand publishing from April 2006). Each title will display a different sticker on the front cover. Collect all 12 throughout the year, stick them on the reverse of the collectors' card which you'll find in *Dancing Dreams* or on the website, download from www.felicitywishes.net. When you have collected all 12 stickers, just send them in to us! In return you'll be entered into a monthly, grand prize draw to receive a very exclusive Felicity Wishes prize*.

Please send in the completed card to the relevant address above and mark it for the attention of...
Felicity Wishes Collectors Competition,
* A draw to pick 50 winners each month will take place from January 2007
- last draw will take place on 30th June 2007.
Prizes will be a Felicity Wishes product which we hope you'll enjoy.
For full terms and conditions visit www.felicitywishes.net/terms